Nobody Here but Me

Judith Viorst   *Pictures by* Christine Davenier

Farrar Straus Giroux ☉ New York

My mom's making phone calls.
My dad's doing e-mail.
My sister's upstairs with her friend.
They're playing great games, but the
    games are for two, not for three.
So even though there are four—count
    them!—four other people right here
    in this house,
It's just as if there's nobody here but me.

—Hey, Mom, can I . . . ?
—Later, sweetie. I'm talking to Grandma.

—Hey, Dad, can you . . . ?
—Later. I'm answering my e-mail.

—Hey, Katie, would you . . . ?
—Go away. No baby brothers allowed.
—I'm not a *baby* brother. I'm a *younger* brother.
—Baby. Younger. Whatever. Go away.

I'm coloring pictures.
I'm drawing a monkey.
I'm dotting red dots on my arms.
I'm painting a heart on the wall, small but blue as can be.
And maybe I'll paint this whole wall. Who would care? With
    all of these people around,
It's just as if there's nobody here but me.

—Hey, Mom. Hello? Hello-oh. Can you hear me?
—Sorry, but I don't want to hear you right now.

—Hey, Dad. Hello? Hello-oh. Can I ask you . . . ?
—Sorry, but I don't want you asking right now.

—Hey, Katie. Couldn't you, just this once . . . ?

—I COULDN'T. Why don't you go get your own friends to play with?

—If that's how you're going to be, then I won't let you be my sister anymore.

—You're making me cry. Boohoo. Now go away.

I'm cutting some nails off.

I'm cutting some hair off.

I'm cutting some fringe off this rug.

I'm cutting a hole in my jeans to make room for my knee.

But I'm not hearing "Stop!" For although there are all these people upstairs and down,

It's just as if there's nobody here but me.

—When are you going to finish talking to Grandma?
—You need to be patient.

—When are you going to finish answering e-mail?
—Can't you be patient?

—When are you going to finish playing dumb games
   with your dumb friend?
—Never.
—Never?
—Never. Now go away.

I'm making a sandwich.

I'm making a fruit drink.

I'm making a chocolate dessert.

And I'm turning our kitchen into a catastrophe.

(That's a really big mess.)

But is someone—is *anyone*—rushing in with the
sponges and mops? Uh-uh.

It's just as if there's nobody here but me.

—I'm hiding, Mom. I'm hiding right this minute.
—I'm not listening.

—I'm hiding, Dad, and you won't be able to find me.
—I'm not listening.

—Okay, Katie, I'm hiding and you won't be able to find
  me and then you'll be sorry you ever said Go away.
—Trust me, I won't be sorry.
—Yes, you will. I know you will.
—I won't. I know I won't. GO HIDE ALREADY!

I'm down in the basement.
I'm scrunched behind boxes.
I've rolled myself up in a ball.
I'm hidden so people could look very hard and not see.
But while I'm waiting for everyone to start calling Where are you?
  Where are you?
It's just as if there's nobody here but me.

—Hey, Mom, are you trying to find me?
(Don't hear an answer.)

—Hey, Dad, are you coming to find me?
(Still no answer.)

—Hey, Katie, I'll give you a hint: Down in the basement.
   Behind all the boxes.
(I don't think she's looking.)
—Why aren't you looking?
(What does a person have to do to get found?)

It's dark in this basement.
It's cold in this basement.
I hate it down in this basement,
And I need to (how can I say this politely?) go pee.
But there isn't even a "shush" when I slam the bathroom door
  VERY LOUDLY.
It's just as if there's nobody here but me.

—Hurry, Mom, I think there's a snake in the shower.
—No, there isn't.

—Hurry, Dad, I think there's a wolf in the hamper.
—No, there isn't.

—Hurry, Katie, I think there's a giant bird with wide black wings
   and it's flapping those wings outside the bathroom window.
—There isn't.
—There is. I know there is. There absolutely is.
—Then why don't you climb on its back and fly away!

I've taken my clothes off.

I've put on my pj's.

I've tucked my own self into bed.

I'm going to sleep without supper or watching TV.

But though I keep yelling Good night, not one single person is
  good-nighting back.

It's just as if there's nobody here but me.

—Zzz zzz.
—I'm done with my phone calls. We could bake a dessert
  for our supper.

—Zzz zzz.
—I'm done with my e-mail. We could ride our bikes before supper.

—Zzz zzz.
—My friend went home. We could work on the jigsaw puzzle till supper.
—Zzz zzz.
—Mom, Dad, come quick. He's in bed. He's asleep. And it isn't his bedtime yet. SOMETHING'S WRONG!

My mom's in my bedroom.
My dad's in my bedroom.
And Katie my sister's here too.
I'm pretending to zzz, but inside I'm going hee-hee.
(That's a mean little laugh.)
They're—all of them—begging, Wake up. But I'm in
   no hurry to open my eyes.
It's just as if . . .
(It serves them right!)
It's just as if . . .
(Too bad for them!)
It's just as if . . .
(But I'm glad that I'm just make-believing)
It's just as if there's nobody here but me.